Dear Parent:

Congratulations! Your child is taking the first steps on an exciting journey. The destination? Independent reading!

STEP INTO READING® will help your child get there. The program offers five steps to reading success. Each step includes fun stories and colorful art. There are also Step into Reading Sticker Books, Step into Reading Math Readers, Step into Reading Phonics Readers, Step into Reading Write-In Readers, and Step into Reading Phonics Boxed Sets—a complete literacy program with something to interest every child.

Learning to Read, Step by Step!

Ready to Read **Preschool–Kindergarten**
• big type and easy words • rhyme and rhythm • picture clues
For children who know the alphabet and are eager to begin reading.

Reading with Help **Preschool–Grade 1**
• basic vocabulary • short sentences • simple stories
For children who recognize familiar words and sound out new words with help.

Reading on Your Own **Grades 1–3**
• engaging characters • easy-to-follow plots • popular topics
For children who are ready to read on their own.

Reading Paragraphs **Grades 2–3**
• challenging vocabulary • short paragraphs • exciting stories
For newly independent readers who read simple sentences with confidence.

Ready for Chapters **Grades 2–4**
• chapters • longer paragraphs • full-color art
For children who want to take the plunge into chapter books but still like colorful pictures.

STEP INTO READING® is designed to give every child a successful reading experience. The grade levels are only guides. Children can progress through the steps at their own speed, developing confidence in their reading, no matter what their grade.

Remember, a lifetime love of reading starts with a single step!

All rights reserved. Published in the United States by Random House Children's Books, a division of Random House, Inc., New York. Originally published in different form in 1968 by Random House Children's Books, New York, with the title *The Early Bird*.

Step into Reading, Random House, and the Random House colophon are registered trademarks of Random House, Inc.

Visit us on the Web!
StepIntoReading.com
randomhouse.com/kids

Educators and librarians, for a variety of teaching tools, visit us at
RHTeachersLibrarians.com

The Library of Congress has cataloged the previous edition of this work as follows:
Scarry, Richard. The early bird / by Richard Scarry.
    p.   cm. — (Step into reading. A step 2 book)
"Adapted from The early bird, 1968 by Richard Scarry."
Summary: After several cases of mistaken identity Early Bird finally finds a worm to play with.
ISBN 978-0-679-88920-5 (pbk.) — ISBN 978-0-679-98920-2 (lib. bdg.)
[1. Birds—Fiction. 2. Worms—Fiction. 3. Animals—Fiction.]
I. Title. II. Series: Step into Reading. Step 2 book.
PZ7.S327Ear   2003   [E]—lcac   2002013879

Printed in the United States of America

15 14 13 12 11 10 9 8 7 6 5

Random House Children's Books supports the First Amendment and celebrates the right to read.

STEP INTO READING

STEP 2

Lowly Worm
Meets
the Early Bird

by Richard Scarry

Published previously as **The Early Bird**

Random House 🏠 New York

The sun
was shining.

Early Bird hopped
out of bed.

He went to the bathroom
and washed his face.

Early Bird
brushed his beak and
combed his feathers.

Then he put on

his blue sailor suit.

Look at what
Early Bird
ate for breakfast!

"Why don't you find a worm
to play with?"
Mommy Bird said.
"What is a worm?"
asked Early Bird.

"A worm wiggles.
It lives in a hole
in the ground,"
said Mommy Bird.

So Early Bird went out
to find a worm.

"Are you a worm?"
asked Early Bird.
"No," said a bug
on a flower.
"I am a ladybug."

"Are you a worm?"
asked Early Bird.

"No, I am a frog,"
said a fat fellow on a log.
"Worms live in holes."

13

Early Bird
saw something
in the ground.
"Are you a worm?"
asked Early Bird.

14

"I am *not* a worm!"
said Bunny Rabbit.
"Worms wiggle all over.
Go look in the garden."

In the garden
Early Bird saw
a wiggly thing.

"Hello, worm,"
Early Bird said.

16

"You mean,
'Hello, mouse tail'!"
said Freddie Field Mouse.

Then he scampered
back into his hole.

Early Bird began to cry.

"What's the matter?"
said a funny fellow.
"I can't find a worm,"
said Early Bird.

"Don't cry,"
said the fellow.
"There's a worm
right over there.
Just hop over
and pull him out."

Early Bird took the worm
in his beak and pulled.

But the worm was stuck
in his hole.

"Give a *big* pull,
Early Bird!"

Pppppop!
"Why, it's you!"
said Early Bird.

"That's right,"
said the fellow.
"My name is
Lowly Worm."

The sun was going down.

Early Bird

had to hurry home

for supper.

"Come with me,"
said Early Bird.
All the way home,
Lowly Worm
and Early Bird
played jump-worm.

They had a good supper.

cuckoo!

Lowly Worm ate
a lot of peas.

Daddy gave Early Bird
and Lowly Worm
a piggyback ride upstairs.

Early Bird took his bath
with a sailboat.
Lowly Worm took *his*
bath with his hat on.

Time to go to sleep!

Early Bird got into bed.

Lowly Worm went to bed

in the flowerpot!

Good night, Lowly Worm!

Good night, Early Bird!